HOW TO RIDE A POLAR BEAR

For Andrew – giant snowballs as promised xx – CH
For Theodore and Nancy xx – EE

SIMON & SCHUSTER

First published in Great Britain in 2018 by
Simon & Schuster UK Ltd
1st Floor, 222 Gray's Inn Road, London WC1X 8HB
A CBS Company

Text copyright © 2018 Caryl Hart (www.carylhart.com)
Illustrations copyright © 2018 Edward Eaves

A CIP catalogue record for this book is available
from the British Library upon request

PB ISBN: 978-1-4711-6291-6   eBook ISBN: 978-1-4711-6292-3
Printed in China   10 9 8 7 6 5 4 3 2 1

HOW TO RIDE A POLAR BEAR

CARYL HART

ED EAVES

SIMON & SCHUSTER

London New York Sydney Toronto New Delhi

At school we are
learning about maps.
We all had to bring one
home to colour in.

I'm still trying to open mine when...

"Albie!"

It's Mum. "How about a trip
to the museum?" she says.

"Do we have to?" I groan.
"Museums are fusty and
dusty and full of smelly
old things!"

But Mum just smiles. "We'll see," she says.
We catch the bus and trundle into town.

At the museum, there's
an Arctic exhibition.
AWESOME!

I try on some furry clothes
and have just started
building an igloo when ...

a snowflake lands on my
nose! HUH? More snow
falls, thicker and faster.

Suddenly ...

"GRRRRRR!"

A huge polar bear
leaps out of the snow!
YIKES!

"Can you help us?" High up on the bear's
back is a girl. "We've got to cross the
frozen sea to get home, but the ice
is melting! Come quick!" she cries.
"B-but I don't know the way!" I stutter.

"We can use your map!" says the girl.
"I'm Yura and this is Tuka," she grins.
We cling to the bear's thick fur and
plunge into the blizzard.

We race through glittering forests, past frozen mountains and through deep snowdrifts. The sky turns from blue to dusky pink. Soon it will be dark.

"We must rest now," says Yura.
"But where will we sleep?" I say.
Yura laughs. "In an igloo of course!"

She shows me how to cut blocks of snow and we build the igloo together.

Then she lights a fire and makes a delicious stew. YUM! We snuggle into warm blankets and soon we are asleep.

But in the middle of the night, a deafening rumble fills the air ...

AVALANCHE!

We dive out of the igloo and
Tuka carries us away, dodging
giant snowballs as they crash
through the trees.

At last we are safe.
But as Tuka pads across the ice, eerie howling fills the valley. Dark shadows slink across the ice towards us.

AROOOOOO!

"Wolves!" cries Yura.

Tuka growls GRRRR! But the wolves
circle closer and closer until ...

SWOOSH!

Something whooshes through the air,
scattering the wolves in every direction.
"What was THAT?" I gasp.
"A good friend!" laughs Yura.

We gather our things
and climb back onto
Tuka. I check the map.
"It's not far now," I say.

But when we reach the sea,
we are too late. "The ice melts
earlier every year!" cries Yura.
"Now we'll never get home!"

Just then, a fountain of water
shoots into the air.

SPLOOSH!

Yura grins, then puts
her hand to her mouth
and whistles ...

When we reach the shore, Yura's
family are waiting for us.

And there's Mum! "So," she grins,
"how was the museum?"

"It was AWESOME!" I say. "And not a fusty, dusty or smelly old thing in sight."

Uh-oh!